Yolanda Grier

Heart in

Pieces

Made Whole

Copyright © Page

Heart in Pieces Made Whole
A Poetic Journey From Trauma and Abuse to Healing and Forgiveness
Copyright © 2020 by Yolanda L. Grier

Table of Contents

Dedication

This book is dedicated to my mother who has taught me so much about love and forgiveness. Often, I witnessed my mother show compassion and concern for families in need. My mother has always had a place in her heart for children. It's a special place that embraces the plight of foster kids and children who need encouragement. I am thankful for the art lessons and for the paper and pencil to write. It is my prayer that we are will continue to thrive and to help others.

Acknowledgments

Thank you, Lord for never leaving me. Thank you for your Holy Spirit guiding me toward the light of your love so that I may hold on just a little while longer. In all of my brokenness, Lord, you reminded me that I was your daughter and that wholeness will be my portion.

To Grier, who has carried my story since before we married and provided the glue until I could find footing, thank you. I am grateful that you caught my tears and loved me even deeper. You walked tall while leading the family with God as your source to show me how to continue to push. I am forever grateful for your continuous support and encouragement.

To the Grier Gang—Kevin, Austin, Sean, Shalanda, and Briana—thank you for being amazing kids and for your love and support while I was writing the book. Your words of encouragement fueled my desire to get this book written. My prayer has always been that my kids witness me thriving in life. God is so faithful.

To my Pastors Tacuma and Dr. Michelle Johnson, I am forever grateful for how you have prayed and fought in the spirit for me. I am forever grateful for the class, Luke 1:38, that helps me to envision a life of freedom from depression and brokenness. Thank you holding my truths safe and for pushing me towards who God would have me to be.

To my mentor, Dr. Saundra Wall Williams, who spoke the words "Move!" I am grateful for your push, your words of wisdom and your desire to see women thrive in their vision and calling from God. I will forever remember the Vision Building Women's Retreat that enabled me to finally write clearly what God had planted in my heart.

To my best friend in the entire world, Sallie B. Stone. I am forever grateful for our friendship since 8th grade. Wow! Look at God. Thanks for the hour-long conversations. Thank you for letting me cry and be imperfect. Thanks for the BOOM retreats to just Breathe. I appreciate all of your questions so that I may hear my own answers. Boomtastic Forever!

Last and certainly not least, this book is for all of the brave survivors of child abuse, rape, molestation and any violation of your spirit. I am cheering for you. I am praying for you. You go this and God's got you.

Preface

"Can't you hear my heart racing
Don't you see me falling apart?
I can't speak
You can't see."

Yolanda Grier

I believe that every time, every-time, every time someone tells their raw, unredacted story, someone else is set free. It is the human equivalent of "Let there be light." It is the most divine, most powerful, most generous, and most spiritual thing that a human being can do. And yet, how many of us have done it?

Have you told your children your story, your raw, unredacted story? Have you told your parents? Your faith community? Your brother or sister? Your mentees? Your mentors? The world?

I haven't.
Yolanda has.
I have had the privilege of being her pastor for a dozen years. We have discussed many things, many times. And yet, as a man, I cannot begin to fathom the righteous bravery that it took for her to pen these words in her journal, much less to publish them for the world to digest.

Her narrative is straightforward, terse, awkwardly and painfully honest. Her poetry is profoundly simple, yet simply profound. A pre-teen can access and understand every word—and yet a person of elder years will surely grapple with the questions that it poses.

Yolanda had the courage to submit this offering from her heart to you. I pray you have the guts to receive it.
To her speaking, to your seeing, to our healing,
Pastor Tacuma Johnson
A People of God

"Grow Fierce!"

I spoke those words to Yolanda years ago. We were in the middle of a process of spiritual, emotional, and physical transformation. What began with a lingering, uncomfortable, healing hug has resulted in an honest, fierce book of truth-telling.

I have no doubt that Yolanda has grown and will continue to grow fierce. These poems testify to her fierceness. I also believe that they will encourage others to grow fierce and to share their testimony.

As you dive into this book, know that every word is intentional. Nothing said, nothing felt, nothing relived is in vain. All things are working together for her good and can work together for your good too.

Dr. Michelle T. Johnson

A People of God

Introduction

I wrote this book of poems because poetry is my language. The Lord gave me this gift. I have written in journals since I was 10 years old. I have loved drawing all of my life. The creative process was already in me. The Lord had already placed inside of me the very thing I would need to find healing in Him. I am extremely grateful.

I wrote this book to remind women that we are brave and courageous. I wrote this book so that we will no longer have to whisper our stories through the weight of judgment, guilt and shame.

I wrote this book for all survivors of abuse, molestation, trauma and depression.

I am who God says I AM. You are as well.

I want you to take a journey with me through poetry. My deepest thoughts and feelings are expressed more easily through poetry.

The poems are divided into five parts:

I Was Breaking -Poems written between ages 15-17

I Was Searching

I Was Hurting

I Was Wandering

I AM HEALED

Chapter 1

I
Was
Breaking

My siblings and I were always singing, dancing, and being creative. My mother taught us to draw and we never ran out of ideas to keep us busy. We played. We fought. We made up. At some it became difficult for me to move on from our fighting. As a sensitive girl who could spend the entire day sitting on the porch reading, arguments and fighting was too much. I didn't like conflict and my stomach would be in knots at the thought of yet another fight.

We really were a regular family on a regular street in a regular town. And something else was regular. I was sad. I was constantly defending myself. I was always afraid. I rarely could fully embrace peace because I knew at some point, I would be in an argument or a fight with my sister. Sibling rivalry is a beast.

My family loved and loved hard. We were close so it appeared everyone was able to get over conflicts pretty quickly. Everyone but me. I felt words very deeply. Certain behaviors created knots in my stomach that I would feel for days. Loud arguments would send vibrations through my body that created anxieties.

I was quiet and very shy as a little girl. I enjoyed playing tetherball, ping pong and kickball. But I quickly reverted back to finding pockets of time to be by myself. I try to stay in the house as much as possible. But my mother would encourage me to go outside and play with the other kids. The truth is that I would have rather been in my room reading and sleeping.

My family agreed with the description of being quiet and shy. But I held a secret that would nearly destroy my life. At age 4, my voice and my innocence were taken by a man named Bennett. Bennett was a tall, medium-frame man who passed out candy to children in the projects. I don't remember having a conversation with him or even going to his apartment for candy. Until...

I was playing in the yards of several apartments with other kids. We were all trying to climb the young tree in his yard. In the projects, many of the small yards were separated by a small sidewalk. Because of the community in which many projects were built, it was not unusual to run and play in several yards at a time.

As we played around the tree and attempted to climb the tree, Bennett came to his screen door and watched for a while. He was cheering all of us to climb higher. When I could climb higher, he continued to encourage us. At one point, he told us he would give candy to whoever could climb the highest.

I was so excited and feeing very confident. I had been climbing higher than most of the kids most of the day. So, I pushed myself with excited energy to climb this tree. The kids on the ground cheered us on and it seem like a good day.

I jump down and ran to Mr. Bennett to get my candy. He pointed to the candy on the stereo console and said I could go get it. As I entered the apartment, he grabbed my hand. I was puzzled. He told me there was more he needed to show me upstairs before I could get the candy. So, I went with him upstairs.

Once we got upstairs and I could no longer hear the sound of the other children and I could no longer see the sunshine from the outdoors, I felt in my spirt that I was trouble. He stood in front of the door and he appeared bigger than life. I kept glancing over the room thinking of a way to get out.

No talking.

Mr. Bennett held me with one hand. There he was fully exposed. The depth of emotions I was experiencing is inexplicable. I couldn't speak. I couldn't scream. Then something startled him. As he negotiated a way to quickly pull his pants up, I dashed past him, down the stairs, grabbed the candy on the stereo console and out the screen door.

The sickness of Mr. Bennett's heart won. Something happened to my soul that day. Something torpedoed my mind and took away innocent thoughts. A part of me left. And the part that remained was crushed. I was left with fear, a stutter, insecurity and a lifetime battle with anxiety and depression. My entire life I could never figure out the words to say to make this make sense.

Set This Little Bird Free

I am in a place

Where I don't want to be

I am like a bird in a cage

And want to be set free

I want to be in a world

Where there's no fussing and fighting

I want the cats and dogs to play

Not always scratching and biting

I want the people to love one another

And I want them to care

I don't want people to be envious

Because I want everyone to share.

There was a time when I just

Wanted to lie down on my bed and die.

But there were so many people

To whom I hadn't said goodbye.

Now I'm in a rowdy world

And I would rather be dead

Anyone reading this may think I'm crazy

But believe what I've said.

I don't need psychological help.

I'm not going out of my mind.

I'm just looking for a place

Where people are sweet, charming, and kind.

I've been suffering for so long

Almost all of my life.

And I'm so sick of living around

Bickering, confusion, and strife.

All these years, I've looked for love.

For a little, but for plenty.

And I've walked up and down these K-town streets

With a smile that has deceived many.

One point in my life, I had enough

Confidence for a whole generation.

Now it's all knocked down,

And nothing's left but the foundation.

It can be rebuilt.

I may even win an award.

But I'm afraid when the job is finished

All the progress will be ignored.

I'm not giving up on life

Even though I'm afraid of what's ahead

One can't begin to think

Of how many nights I've cried in bed.

So, I guess I'll sit back

And see what life holds for me.

And hope someone will come

To set this little bird free.

If I could leave

And go to a faraway place

I'd leave this very moment

As if I were in a race.

If I could leave

I'd never come back

Because there's nothing here for me

And everyone is slack.

If I could leave

I'll leave without one goodbye

There won't be a tear, a mourn

A saddened face or a sigh.

A smile

A laugh

A sigh

A frown

A deep hurt

Pain

Like a baby

The sinner

Weeps his prayer to God

Is God listening?

Death

Cold, dark

Creeping, crawling, coming

He always follows his victim

Shadow!

Patiently

Humbly

Readily

The Lord

Awaits

My wandering soul

Salvation

My plea to God

God, I am tired of living in sin

And paying an unearned fee.

Please God! Oh please!

Come and take me back with Thee.

Step into my world

And share my world with me

Step into my world

I promise you'll be free

Free from constant bickering

Strife, misery and shame

Free from all hatred

Heartache, war and pain

Step into my world

And you shall surely see

A Heavenly Father sitting up high

Watching over me.

I saw that dark and cold shadow today

Walking around my bed

He looked me straight in my eyes

And boldly, yet hesitantly said,

"I don't want you to be afraid.

I just want your soul."

I blinked and blinked hoping he'll disappear

But there he stood, mighty and bold.

If only I had a heart

I would be able to sing

And talk about all the things

That love brings.

If only I had a heart

I would be able to love

And tell everyone about

My Father above

If only I had a heart

And not an empty space

Maybe I would not be rusty

And just a big waste.

I sat up in my bed

Gasping for air like a trout

Then out of my mouth, slowly but surely came,

"In the name of Jesus, cast out!"

He disappeared in the night

I felt humble and free

From his hectic grasp and cold, dark voice

Why does he always haunt me?!

Like an airplane

My life

Flies by rapidly

Is there another flight soon?

Journal Reflections

Have you ever experienced hurt inflicted by a person in authority?
Using your 5 senses, describe the situation?

_____

_____

_____

_____

_____

_____

_____

_____

_____

_____

_____

_____

Are there areas in your life that you desire to grow more fiercely?
What does that look like?

_____

_____

_____

_____

_____

_____

_____

_____

_____

_____

_____

Has God ever delivered you from a harmful situation or relationship? How did you grow from the experience?

_____

_____

_____

_____

_____

_____

_____

_____

_____

_____

_____

_____

Chapter 2

I
Was
Searching

I tried to put this moment behind me and I find solace in writing and drawing. I would cry most nights and some days. It felt good to sleep most of the time. I found myself crying when my family would wake me up to eat. I just wanted to read, write and sleep. I cried in church. I cried in the classroom. I cried on the playground. I cried watching certain TV shows. Soft music made me cry. I cried myself to sleep.

As a young girl, I remember loving to go to church. My siblings and I enjoyed the youth groups, the choirs and many other activities the church offered. I particularly loved being with the older women of the church. They were so matter-of-fact. I was intrigued by their different hair styles and the creative ways they would dress up, since jewelry and make-up weren't allowed for me.

I learned to love the Bible and spent a great amount of time reading it. Admittedly, reading the King James version of the Bible keep me perplexed so I would often use a dictionary for words I didn't understand.

I had a great respect and admiration for our youth pastor—Pastor Parham. I grew to love him as a father. He was married to the sweetest soul of a woman and was a father to four daughters. They always made me feel like I was a part of the family.

Our youth department planned a trip to Jones Lake and everyone was excited to go. I remember going to the lake with my family. I imagined this trip being just as fun.

The lake was filled with kids from other districts as it was a major outing for the churches. Some of the kids were diving off the pier and many were in the water closer to the shore. I noticed a line of kids having fun diving in the water. I quickly realized the men were teaching the kids to dive. The line got shorter and now it was my term.

There was one man on either side of me. I was to place a foot in each of their hands and squat done so that they could catapult me through the air. I knew Brother Leo and Brother Wade. So, nothing stirred in my spirit. Until…

As the moment I squatted, I immediately noticed they didn't immediately push me up from the water. They both pushed their fingers inside of my bathing suit. As I fought to get away one of their fingers injured me inside. I was in shock. I ran out of the water still in shock not knowing what to say or where to go. The lake was filled with so many faces that was familiar and many who weren't.

I ran all over the park looking for Pastor Parham. I found him standing at a picnic table talking to a group of people. I ran all of the way and now I was speechless. I sat at the picnic table and just watched him trying to figure out what I was going to say. I remember him stopping and asking if I were ok. I don't remember how I responded exactly. I remember thinking who is going to believe me if anyone would believe me if I told them two leaders of the church tried to put their fingers in me, a girl 14 years old.

I decided to try and forget it and push the moment way back in my mind.

I'm broken and I know it

Pieces on the ground

Scattered all around

Soft steps not to despair

Not to disrupt

Not to know

But yet I sit quietly

Waiting for you to acknowledge me

Don't you see me?

Can't you hear my heart racing

Don't you see me falling apart?

I can't speak

You can't see.

The room appears large

As the curtains are closed

A bed that stands steep

He is exposed

Something's not right

Tall doorway is blocked

I am 4 years old

Frightened, anxious, shocked.

I can't scream

I don't cry

I know I must run

With wings I could fly

A brief moment of escape

I must take it now

I'll fly past him

And not worry about how

I'm running to be free

From the clutches of his hand

Now a lifetime of pain

This can't be God's plan.

Sitting on the couch

Curtains catching the sun

He looks back and smiles

I know I only have to run

He said "She's Yolanda"

My daughter, a quiet soul

Feeling immeasurably loved

My life seemed in control.

There is he standing
Larger than life
He's smart and courageous
I'll grow to be his wife

No! tangled with other
Harsh words and refrain
That's your Dad
You should feel ashamed

Failed to communicate
I feel safe and loved
You lack understanding
Nasty fits you like a glove

I don't understand
Why you get to be mean
You exist with no rules
I just want to scream

But who would hear
The sounds of my heart
Breaking in tiny pieces
I'm Ok. I'm Smart.

Holiday lights and cheer

Overwhelm my soul

This feeling is intense

My heart is not cold

What to do with a doll

I have no clue

Should I hug or talk to her?

Short, tall, pink, same hue?

I'll just let her be

Even if she's probably fun

I look to the north

Because I just want to run

You could hug me

We could go hang out

But you would rather hit me

Ignore me and pout

Would anyone notice

If I disappeared in the Neuse

Life is very busy

Under the pine, maple and spruce

Sounds of laughter

Fill the playground at dawn

I should leave now

Don't want to be hopped on

Why did you hit

Always afraid, always sad

No one sees me

I wonder if they're glad

Standing tall and blonde

I loved her so

My 3rd grade teacher

She always had a glow

She always offered a hug

Or a shoulder to catch our tears

Our being made her smile

With loud laughter and cheers

Ms. Powers shared her love

With the entire class

Though I felt so special

Through my looking glass.

Bricks red and playground large

School was a lot of fun

Unless it was a day

I felt I had to run

Running was not an option

Trouble was everywhere

Mean girls in the streets

Strange men in the air

Journal Reflections

Describe what peace of mind means to you.

_____

_____

_____

_____

_____

_____

_____

_____

_____

_____

_____

Write about a time in which you prayed, you waited and God answered.

_____

_____

_____

_____

_____

_____

_____

_____

_____

_____

_____

What are your thoughts about true peace?

Chapter 3

I
Was
Hurting

At some point I wasn't thinking about what I happened in Mr. Bennet's bedroom or what happened at Jones Lake. I was trying to pretend like everything in my world was okay. Until one summer day I was walking home from Ms. Lily's house. Ms. Lily was an elderly lady I agreed to sit with at night. Knowing how much I loved being around older women, my Aunt Ollie asked if I would sit with Ms. Lily. I would stay overnight and listen to her as she moaned and cried out in prayer to God because she would be in pain. Often times she would ask me to rub her back with alcohol.

Ms. Lily's home was filled with several pictures of Jesus Christ hanging on the walls throughout. The home was a shotgun house in which you could walk straight from the front of the house to the back. I felt safe there. And even more enjoyable—she didn't require much talking from me.

As I walked from her home that summer morning, my cousin saw me and asked where I was coming from. I told him. He insisted for another answer.

He seemed annoyed, thinking I was lying to him. So, he decided he would walk home with me to make sure my mother knew I was coming in the house in the early morning hours. I found myself in the house with him, as my mother was at work. I remember him going to the bathroom and then stopping by my bedroom. My mother frowned upon guests running back and forth to the bathroom and she was clear that no males, including cousins, were to ever enter our bedrooms. So instantly this felt uneasy.

He yelled out for me to come to the bedroom so that he could talk about the art and poetry on my wall. I told him he should leave. He agreed, pulled out a joint and started walking towards the door. I asked him to put the joint away because that wasn't allowed in our house.

He put the joint away and as his hands came back out of the pocket, he grabbed me and tried to pull me towards him. It happened so quickly. Soon I found myself fighting to keep him off of me. So

40

many thoughts were running through my head. He was overpowering me when a brass candelabra that my mother had for years caught my eye.

The candelabra spent most of the time as a wall decoration. Because my mother rearranged the home very often, it was now on the table. So with my loose hand I grabbed it and with everything in me I began to hit him. I wasn't sure where I was hitting him. I knew I couldn't stop swinging.

He immediately left. I carried such a sick feeling in my stomach. What kind of sick mind could desire a cousin? And again, why do men think it's okay to just take? Why does this keep happening? Are all men like this? Is my body for the pleasure of a man who can just take at any moment? Lord, help me.

I would like to tell you that these are my only experiences, but that wouldn't be true. I want to tell you that I was able to push the memories way back in my mind, and that my childhood ended up being one of skipping through meadows and singing in the rain all the time.

I have struggled with being okay most of life. I thought I was alone until I began to share my story. And it absolutely blew my mind when I realized how pervasive it was in many families and communities for men to prey on little girls, and even sometimes women preying on little boys.

The long walk home

Tension in the air

She knows where I've been

Does she know who was there?

He invited me in

And promised me a treat

He watched all afternoon

In his framed box seat

The laughter of children

In the air of innocence

While he locked his attention

Attracted to winsomeness

Danger waited for me

At the top of the steps

Age 4, alone with a man

Tall, dark, scary, biceps

Sitting in the shadow

Lurking in a whim

Don't know who it is

Wonder if it's him

Adults roaming all around

Many going to and fro

If I pretend to be asleep

Will they turn around and go?

I hear a whisper

"That's the one laying on the bed"

Two or three grown men staring

Silence. Nothing will be said.

What are you looking for

In the shadow of the night?

Lurking in the hallway

While the room is filled with fright?

Lord please help me

Not to breathe loudly or move

The men may enter the room
And use my little body to soothe.

I don't want to hug you
Yet still you insist
Embrace my young body close
So you can enjoy the kiss

What could you be thinking?
People just stare
This is not normal to do
Doesn't anyone care?

Notice how my face cringes
How each hand is now a fist
My arms strained tightly
Pushing away to resist

I can't seem to say, "No"
Adults seem to be okay
Something needs to change
I think I will run away.

Long walks in the park
Green grass all around
Tall trees happily blowing
Leaves dancing to the ground.

The track is a staple
For many around town
I love the freedom it brings
I no longer feel bound

The air here seems different
Fresh and open in a way
The sun is about to set
So, sadly I can't stay

Walks in the park
To clear my mind from pain
To allow my tears to fall
And drift to the Adkin Canal's drain

Bag under the bed
Loosely packed, pushed out of view
As long as I remain quiet
People in my room will be few

Planning an escape
To the edge of no where
A mental log in my heart
Of names who would care.

I have no money
That is a concern
I could pack plenty of food
Perishable, nothing to burn

I can't get up

Feels like a rock holding me down

All night crying

Too many people around

I want to sleep the day away

Don't want to go to school.

Children playing and having fun

If I speak, I might be rude.

I drag myself out

To push through one Monday

I pray often to God

To please make a way

Journal Reflections

Is there anyone in your life who needs your forgiveness? Write a prayer.

_____

_____

_____

_____

_____

_____

_____

_____

_____

_____

Is there anyone in your life you need to forgive? Ask God for strength. Write His response.

_____

_____

_____

_____

_____

_____

_____

_____

_____

_____

Using the 5 senses, describe forgiveness.

_____

_____
_____
_____
_____
_____
_____
_____
_____
_____
_____

Chapter 4

I
Was
Wandering

I shared my story in church settings, in school settings and even at work. But what always broke my heart was as soon as I told my story and began to exit, a woman would find her way to me and whisper her story. She would cry, saying "You told my story!" Or I would often hear, "I have never told anyone." How could this be? Why is the weight of shame, guilt, and humiliation so heavy? And who can help lift this burden that keeps many of us silent?

My answer came when I heard these words, "Mrs. Grier, may I tell you something, I am being molested at home." There she stood, a girl about 11 years of age. Her face was soft and her eyes clear. Her hair was unkept and her clothes weren't tidy. She immediately asked that I not tell but to try and figure out a way to get her out of the home. We both knew she couldn't have one without the other. I immediately reported it and soon an investigation ensued.

Her confiding in me believing that something would happen awakened something in me. It always saddened me when I realized that even if my particular experiences weren't known, many people knew about the behavior of the men I mentioned. And because of that I became resentful.

Why protect them? Why was predatory behavior allowed to run rampant in some communities and even some churches? I was baffled—there are no easy answers to these questions.

No longer could I push the stories of the ladies who whispered their stories. I couldn't get the image of the young girl out of my mind. And then something amazing and pivotal happened. Within two weeks, three of the men who had molested and violated me when I was a girl, sent me a Face Book friend request. I could barely breathe! The audacity—it had been decades! Are you kidding me? What did they want? Did they think I had forgotten? I had no say in who was family or what church I attended as a girl. Yet, I could control who gets to be in life now.

And for the first time in my life, I was able to experience the one emotion that I was never comfortable with. Anger. As a youth I watched a lot of people live and make decisions in anger. I heard words spoken in anger. The power of angry actions and angry words were like superpowers of damaged lives. So I had tried to remove it from my arsenal of survival tools.

Yet in that moment, a righteous rage surged in me. I spoke out loud to myself about what I had endured. I cried rivers of tears that seem to have no end. I thought about my stolen innocence. It angered me that as a woman my voice meant little. And once I got over myself and acknowledged my anger, I prayed "Lord, I want to see in me what you see. I need Your help."

As I sit in the tree

The world seems so vast

I wonder to myself

"How long will this last"

I am slow to speak

Since no one hears

I cry at night

A pillow absorbs my tears

Tears of anger

Tears of pain

Tears of loneliness

Tears of shame

The tree seems safe

Green leaves and even bugs

If I climb down

Will I get a hug?

Unseen in plain sight

As I sit in the tree

Afraid of the unknown
Yet I desire to be free

Anybody out there
Does anyone care
This world is confusing
Drowning in clean air

Sitting in a tree
I know the world's in his hands
Lord, can you hear me
Not sure how much I can stand

The night is quiet with sudden movements

Interrupts my rest

Is this yet another dream

One that leave my chest tight

I am lonely with a house

Full of movements

Some quick, some reactive

All painful

Can you see me?

Really see me?

Do you hear the sniffles?

Notice the tears on the pillow

Anyone there

The night is quiet with sudden movements

Stomach aching and chest tightening

Can hardly breathe

I just want to be

Be happy

Be loved

Be noticed

Be complimented

Belong

I want to love

I want to trust

My heart always aches

Shhh…hush…

That sound in the head

Secrets in my soul

No one to save me

This world remains so cold

Look in my eyes

Small tender and sweet

This man tall and strong

four years old, I am weak

I ran and ran

Toward the sound of my name

Ten minutes to devour innocence

A lifetime of shame

Now broken, weak, scared

Quiet invisible to most

No skipping, no laughing

No one can get close

I want to love

I want to trust

My heart always aches

Shhh…hush…

I wonder what you saw

When I cried on the floor

I wonder what you saw

When I begged you to stay

Did you hear the loud break?

My heart in despair

Did you notice my little hand?

Pleading with dare

Sunrising, silhouette leaving

Intense indescribable feeling

Scared to be alone...again

Sitting on the couch not sure why

Calm morning, gentle smile

I feel loved and adored

I hope this last awhile.

Blue-green curtains allowing a little sun

As you look upon my face

No words, a half smile

I felt safe in this space

Night cold and movements are deliberate

Footed pajamas, coats and trikes.

It's time to go…but where?

In the cover of night, a caravan of kids

Silence, no words, just go

Feeling anxious and calm all in one

She'd lead. We'll follow.

We'll all be safe.

Sleeping on the floor.

She sleeps in the bed.

Awakened to moisten bottom.

Yet I know I am dry.

Why did she pour water

And tell a lie?

Now again, no one believes

My alibi

Sleep

She did it.

She always did.

No one sees

No one cares.

Hit her, why don't you.

You want me to cause pain.

I can't hurt what I love

There will be retribution and shame

Hit her while I hold her down.

I see how you're treated

Yes, everyone does

Just tired of feeling defeated

So, I will continue to

Fight for peaceful rest

Continue to wait on the smile

Continue to wait on the love

The air is always tensed

The sounds of life do exist

So much living going on

Some is sealed with a kiss

Christmas lights and toys galore

Time for merry and cheer

But I can't fully engage

My little body speaks fear

Just the right word

And certainly, the right move

Would render me silent

Because nothing could I prove

I see a glimpse of hope

My aunt loves me so

She brought me a rainbow umbrella

So my tears won't flow

Fire helps destroy

Things that are trash

My eyes can't believe

My toys are in that stash

Balloons and peppermint cake

Let the festivities begin

Family friends and food are here

All to my chagrin

Happy and stress butterflies

All in the same moment

Because after this is over

In the night, my opponent.

The man with the camera

Is happy just to be

His presence knots my stomach

He's looking down at me

The sun is shining

Though it missed my life

My voice has silenced

Worry, anxiety and strife

Gifts come with overwhelm

Holidays are long

I wish I could tell

I just hold on to a song

He touched me

And made me whole

I heard it while in church

Trying to get tears under control

Tears, tears and more tears

All I do is cry

My pillow is a river

What happens if I die?

Special doesn't apply

Neither does pretty or cute

A seed of rejection

Will yield the same fruit.

I open my mouth

My words seem to betray

I want the world to know

What happened that day.

Someone always knows
The coming and going in the hood
The gatekeeper of the projects
Without a doubt understood

Some are to be protected
Some things we are to hide
Don't mess up his reputation
For his family, he provides.

Other girls entered and left
Protectors turned their heads
They whispered sad stories
And slept soundly in their beds

Standing in the shower

Baring my soul

The water will hide the tears

The Lord only knows

I can hardly maneuver

In a world filled with despair

I want to feel love

So I know you care.

Hugs don't feel safe

Hiding out of sight

Some say I'm shy

The truth…I have no fight

I found words!

Words in a brown book

Heaven on earth

That was my hook

Within the bound covers

Where life and death

My wings were lifting

I was given my breath

Figuring how to say

The stirring in my heart

Yet fear, guilt, and shame

Wouldn't let me start.

Some I hold on

To the words that I write

My heart isn't as heavy

There actually may be light

Sitting on the pew

Hoping no one sees

The tears marching on my face

I wish I could freeze

Why did the elder squeeze my hand?

Let me go. Just let me go

The wife frowns upon me

I'm 13. What do I know?

Could I talk to you madam

And tell you my story

Will you hate me?

Or teach me about His glory?

Journal Reflections

Write about a time in which you experienced conflicting emotions?

_____

_____

_____

_____

_____

_____

_____

_____

_____

_____

What are your thoughts about joy and happiness?

_____

_____

_____

_____

_____

_____

_____

_____

_____

_____

Is there someone you could write a prayer for right now?

_____

_____

_____

_____

_____

_____

_____

_____

_____

_____

Chapter 5

I

AM

Healed

If you are still here, thank you for holding the hand of a little girl as she traveled this journey again. It is not always easy to retell hurtful stories. Yet, it is in the telling of our stories that we find healing. It is in the telling of our stories that God is gloried. I am absolutely who God says I AM.

My heart has been healed. I have forgiven those who hurt me. I may receive an apology. You may never receive an apology. Our healing is attacked to allowing God to be God.

Matthew 6:33 NIV reads "But seek first His kingdom and his righteousness, and all these things will be given to you as well." This scripture verse saved my life. I began seeking God instead of seeking acceptance from people, approval from people, and permission from people.

God bless all of those who intended to harm me. I pray that you allow God to heal your brokenness and to turn from ways that are evil. I pray that God heals your heart and fills it with things that are good.

"But I say unto you, Love your enemies, bless them that curse you, do good to them that hate you, and pray for them which despitefully use you, and persecute you." Matthew 5:44 NIV

Tears rolling down my face

To their nightly destination

As I cry out to my Lord

Waiting on His revelation

My pillow isn't as soaked from

Catching my warm tears

I feel my heart a little lighter

Refreshed after all these years.

He's that kind of friend

This I know for sure

I am holding on to His promises

These I know will endure.

I surrender this pain to You

I want to trust and obey

I see things happening around me

Lord, please have your way

I fall prostrate in your presence

I have nothing to lose

I give you my heart Lord

Because life I did choose

Fill my cup Lord

With all things good

I write this prayer to you

You always understood

You blessed my hands

To create using words

I no longer want to fly away

Like the blue and red birds

Words have power

And so, I turn my life around

I choose life and not death

Because the tongue is profound

I am never alone

So many lies were told

You didn't make a mistake

I stand bare and bold.

I carry no more shame

You empowered my hands with art

My Creator placed a gift inside

Hidden deep in my heart

To protect the very gift

That will open up my world

To glorify the Lord

From an irritant to a pearl

A world of words, images and color

To tell the word "I AM"

My mind is renewed

My life no longer a sham.

Because He Lives

My days are filled with hope

I can remember the jack rocks,

Basketball and jumping ropes.

I bow down to pray

Not to hold myself in pain

I await all things that are great

Lord, send the rain.

Tears on the altar
Where I know I am safe
Eyes closed to the world
While I run this race.

I felt so close to You
Lord, I knew you were near
I surrendered my all
Trusting You, no fear.

Learning to be courageous
In Your image I am made
No unforgiveness in my heart
All of my sins you forgave.

Thank you, Lord, for healing me
So that I may soar
The world is not so scary
Life no longer feels like a chore.

Colors and textures,
I didn't notice before
Seem to capture my soul
As they never had before

It's as if I hear
A still small voice
Gently reminding me
That I have a choice

Warm yellows dancing
Chasing the cool blues
Subtle tints that tantalize
With captivating bright hues

I feel my heart open
To something so real
No more hurt and confusion
My life's about to change.

My Lord, My God

You delivered me!

My heart was broken.

And you set me free.

Tears of joy

Streaming down my face

I couldn't see

While my trust was displaced.

I won't let go

I won't go back

I thirst for your love

You kept me intact.

Inside I break and ache

It's a daily to-do

Cries in my heart

I wish someone knew

Inside I break and ache

Confusing as it may sound

Everyone knew his name

Well known around town

Inside I break and ache

Let's just mind our own lane

We talk in soft whispers

To avoid the talk and shame

But God took my heart

Gently, piece by delicate piece

To put it together again

To ensure I had relief.

So now I break this chain

And I ache no more

I pray strength for all others

To receive the peace God has in store.

To God be the Glory

Great things He hath done

He mended my broken heart

No longer do I run

I'm courageous and brave

Because of the Great I AM

I love and mind my self-talk

In the bush there was a ram

I have nothing to give

Yet I owe my life

God allowed me to be

A mother of five and a wife

He loves me so much

He made no mistake

My story was a journey

But I didn't break.

Thank You Lord! Thank You Lord!

My soul cried out!

I am whole and complete

Beyond a shadow of a doubt.

You wouldn't let me drown.

They have no power over me.

I am a whole, healed, delivered

I AM finally FREE!!

Journal Reflections

What does "being whole and complete" mean to you?

_____
_____
_____
_____
_____
_____
_____
_____
_____
_____
_____

Write about ways you can grow through adversity?

_____

_____

_____

_____

_____

_____

_____

_____

_____

_____

_____

Imagine thriving in your life and calling.

_____

_____

_____

_____

_____

_____

_____

_____

_____

_____

We made it. Together. Thank you for taking this journey with me.

 It is my prayer that God will grant you the desires of your heart. That He will lift every burden and set you free from any situation that stands between your calling and Him. I pray that your heart will be lifted with joy everlasting. I pray that peace will be granted to you and your life becomes a beacon for others.

In Jesus Name

Amen

Your final thoughts

_____

_____

_____

_____

_____

_____

_____

_____

_____

_____

_____

_____

_____

About the author

Yolanda Grier is a writer, mixed-media artist and art educator who lives in High Point, North Carolina. Yolanda is a 1986 graduate of North Carolina A&T State University. Yolanda believes strongly in the healing power of writing and creating art. Her belief is deeply rooted in her own healing.

Yolanda teaches art journaling, soul journaling and art classes so that others may experience freedom. Art provides a way for the heart to communicate and to find healing.

Yolanda is available for teaching, speaking and creating.

info@yolandagrier.com

Facebook – Treasure Heart Creative

Instagram- Treasure_Heart_Creative

YouTube-Treasure Heart Creative

About the book:

After struggling with depression and anxiety for years, Yolanda discovered the creative gift inside of her that provided a place to creatively heal. The effects of abuse, molestation and trauma became strongholds. Yolanda's life bears witness for others to see the fruit of forgiveness. The fruit she desired was to thrive in life. In Heart In Pieces Made Whole, Yolanda takes the reader on a poetic journey from trauma to healing. The poems were taken from childhood journals to the current writings.

Made in the USA
Middletown, DE
09 September 2020

19321133R00064